The Princess and the Pea

Written by
Stephen Rickard

Illustrated by
Dynamo

Once upon a time there was a charming prince.
He was called Prince Casper.

Casper wanted to marry a princess.

After all, he was a prince. He could not marry just anybody!

Prince Casper looked all over the kingdom for a princess.

He found many princesses, but every time something was not right. Prince Casper did not think that any of the girls he met was a true princess.

Prince Casper was unhappy.

How could he find a true princess?

One night the prince was at home with the king and queen in the royal castle.

Outside there was a big storm. The rain rained and the wind blew. There was even thunder and lightning.

Then there was a sudden knocking.

A girl was standing outside. She looked very wet and cold.

"Can I shelter from the rain?" asked the girl.
"I am a princess."

The king asked the girl to step inside. Yes, she could shelter for the night.

"I wonder," said Prince Casper to the queen. "Is she a true princess?"

The queen wanted to find out.

The queen went to the bedroom.

She put a little pea under the mattress. Then she put another 20 mattresses on the bed. Then she put the sheets and the blankets back on top.

That night the princess slept in the bed.

The next morning, the king, the queen and Prince Casper asked the girl if she had slept well.

"No," said the girl. "I had a very bad sleep. The bed was very lumpy. I am black and blue all over."

Prince Casper, the king and the queen were happy. This was good news.

Now they knew that the girl was a true princess.

So the prince asked the girl to be his wife.

They had a huge wedding and the prince and princess were very happy.

And where is the pea?

They put it in a museum.

It is still there, unless somebody has taken it!